HEGARTY AND THE
DOLEFUL DANCER

HEGARTY AND THE DOLEFUL DANCER

Leon Murphy

LARGE
PRINT

First published in 2007 by
Sandstone Press
This Large Print edition published
2009 by BBC Audiobooks
by arrangement with
Sandstone Press Ltd

ISBN 978 1 405 62246 2

British Library Cataloguing in Publication Data available

Printed and bound in Great Britain by
CPI Antony Rowe, Chippenham, Wiltshire

For Asti

CHAPTER ONE

THE JADE BUDDHA

My name is Daniel Hegarty. I am a private detective and an alcoholic.

Those two things are important to remember. I mean they're important things for *me* to remember. Any crisis and I might slip. I have before. High stress can also push me over. Four years is not long on the wagon. My job means that long stretches of boredom are broken up by near death adventures. There's stress for you.

It's a long time since I forgot my name but it has happened.

I am forty-two years of age. Marie and I are divorced now, and we never speak. I shouldn't have drunk so much but she shouldn't have gone out with that other guy. I shouldn't have shouted and thrown that big punch at her. When it missed she stepped forward and—*bop!*—jabbed me on the chin. All of a sudden I was sitting on the carpet looking up at her and Dermot. Marie had her hands over her mouth and her eyes were wide. She was shocked at what she had done.

Look at me sitting on the carpet one way and it is comedy. Look at me another and it is tragedy. This is what it is to be a drunk—half clown, half sad actor.

Dermot is our son. He put himself between us and I sobered up. He was just thirteen at the time. The damage was done and it was time to move out. That was six years ago.

I'll tell you what it feels like with Marie. It feels like God soaked a big white duvet in an icy river and threw it over us. All either of us feels is this cold sensation. We can't move because it holds us down. As long as it sits over us we can't really connect with anyone else. It keeps us apart

2

and it keeps us on our own. Marie's boyfriend is long since gone from her life. I wish she could have loved him. It would have been a sort of ending.

Dermot is at university now. He sides with his mother but he tries to understand. He forgives me. He is the warm spot in my soul.

Now I live in a one room rented flat round the corner from my office. The office is a two room job in Grove Street, just opposite the Grove Bar, not far from Gordongrove Park. Over the years I put a lot of money into the Grove's bank account.

Sarah Bush, my PA, sits in reception and does very little work. Since schooldays she has been called 'Sugar'. She says she will only stay until something better comes along.

*   *   *

One day, not too long ago, I was standing at the window. Snitch

3

Mitchell had just disappeared through the doors of the Grove. Snitch was wearing his usual brown raincoat, with trainers and a baseball cap. He wears them to blend in, he says. Snitch has a very long nose which he strokes with his finger when he listens. Since his game is to listen and tell he strokes it a lot. When he blows it he takes a big blue handkerchief out of his pocket and honks into it four, maybe five times. When he finishes he uses it to give the nose a polish, back and forth. Over the years it has picked up a high shine.

No one who knows him would miss him in a crowd. But he usually has his ear to the ground. I was sure he could tell me something about Big McBride.

Word on the streets was that Big McBride had been moved out of High Security in Her Majesty's Hotel by the Sea. Soon he would be placed in an open prison nearer home. He was on his way to freedom.

Big was one of those large scale convicts who put on weight in prison. Snitch said he had screws as personal servants. When they arrived in the great man's limo visitors would be led inside to a cell which was apart from all the others. Big had been given his own private place in what was called 'isolation'. This meant he was safe from harm and could do more or less what he liked. The screws turned a blind eye to the visitors he used to control his criminal empire.

Inside he ate like a king and had plenty of brandy and cigars. Word had it that lady visitors were allowed to stay over. Since he still controlled most of the businesses in the city where you could hire these ladies, there would be plenty who could pay him a call.

News of his release would not be welcome to his old business partner, Precious Emanuel. Precious had fingered Big to the police on VAT returns. From inside Big had had a couple of Precious's men sliced up and dropped in the river. But he had left Precious himself alone. Everyone knew Big wanted Precious Emanuel done 'special like'.

The police would have been quite happy for these two to take each other out. They could tidy up the small fry in their own time.

I had a couple of hours to kill before meeting a new client at the Museum, a woman named Lindi Lomax. The Museum was her choice. I took out my mobile phone and pressed Snitch's number. It was filed under 'Simon Martin' in case the phone fell into the wrong hands. It wouldn't do for Big, Precious or the police to know he fed me information.

'Yah!' he said.

'It's Dan. Got time?'

'Be right up.'

As I turned the phone off Sugar

6

entered with the day's mail, as usual without knocking. Sugar is a few years older than me. A divorcee, she likes musicals on DVD, nights out with her friends. Home cooking, white wine and vodka have made her broad in the beam, but comfortably so. She has no permanent attachments. She often tells me she has given up on permanence, but I sometimes see her looking at me wistfully.

'Are you remembering you have to meet Ms Lomax later?'

'Sure. She doesn't want to come here. That's what she told you, right?'

'That's right,' she said, looking at the envelopes in her hand. 'You've got some bills here, also this little brown parcel. And this letter looks like your son's handwriting.'

I opened Dermot's letter first.

'He's left home,' I said. My first thought was that this was good. I would get to see him more often.

'Fallen out with Mum?'

'Nah. Just wants more freedom. He's sharing a flat with—Karen.'

'Oh-hoh!'

I dropped Dermot's note on my desk.

'Don't disapprove, Dan. He's nineteen. What else should he be interested in?'

If he's like me at the same age the answer is 'drink'. In a better world I would call Marie to talk it through.

At this point Snitch arrived. He took his baseball cap off when he entered. With Sugar present he would play the gentleman. 'I'll leave you two to it,' she said.

'You smell of beer, Snitch,' I told him.

'Just the one, Mr Hegarty—does me all day.'

We sat on opposite sides of my desk and his watery, sunken eyes played across my papers and diary. They lingered on the little brown parcel.

'I hear Big McBride is being moved,' I said.

'He'll be out in six months, Mr Hegarty.'

'Precious Emanuel can't be pleased.'

'Right now he's more worried about an item missing from his collection.'

Precious got his nickname from the collection of rare and historical art he had collected over the years. His speciality was really old stuff, statues without arms, religious icons, that kind of thing. They said his penthouse was full of them.

'If I know Precious, half the collection will be hot. He'll want to keep the police at arm's length. Who gets close, Snitch?'

'Cleaners, people like that. His lawyers go there. Maybe a few close operatives. He had a girlfriend but she left.'

'Did she now?'

'A woman called Lindi Lomax, a

pole dancer.'

'She'll be uncomfortable just now.'

'Maybe she will, Mr Hegarty.'

'So what's gone missing?'

'It's a jade Buddha from 14th century China. It's priceless.'

'Someone is going to hurt for this.'

'The word is everywhere. Anyone trading for this is in the brown stuff. He wants it back.'

'I'll bet. All of a sudden, Precious looks vulnerable. Big McBride must be laughing in his open prison. Which side are you on, Snitch?'

'Yours, Mr Hegarty, you know that.'

'But you go with the wind. Do you know the word "equilibrium", Snitch?'

'Sure, it means everything balances. Everything is going along evenly and nothing is too strong for anything else or rocking the boat.'

'That's changing. Stay in touch?'

'Will do.'

Snitch left and I opened the little

brown parcel. The postmark said it had been posted locally. It was neatly wrapped and sealed with tape. I had to take a pair of scissors to it. Inside the brown paper was a cardboard box. I opened it, took out what was inside and laid it on my desk in front of me. It was a little green statue of a fat guy dressed in robes and sitting cross legged on the ground.

Unlike me he seemed pretty content. I put him into the drawer where I keep my Colt Police Special and box of bullets.

CHAPTER TWO

CHLOROFORM

Stookie Frampton was at the hamburger stall beside the Museum's back door. I waited until his back was turned before running upstairs and inside to the window beside the door.

The man was not wearing a jacket and his shirt sleeves were rolled up. He was very tall with a big chest and shoulders and had tattoos. I could make out a commando knife on his right arm but not the writing.

It was Stookie all right, Precious Emanuel's bodyguard. I wondered if he had seen me, and why he was here.

About a year before, Sergeant Hammer of the CID had paid me to follow Stookie. Sam Hammer sometimes did this. He knew I would bend the rules where his own detectives would not. If things went wrong he would blame me. This time he had wanted to link Stookie with the East End protection racket. If he could do that he thought he might get something on Precious Emanuel as well.

Stookie had turned into a dark alley behind the Park Hotel. I should have stayed outside and waited. Instead I followed. He was crouched in a corner. When I passed he stepped out and tapped me on the shoulder. My heart jumped into my mouth.

'Well, Hegarty,' he said. 'You should know better.'

He reached into his jacket and his hand closed on something. I wasn't waiting to find out what. I grabbed one of the hotel's bins, pulled off the lid and turned it over his head. Left-over food, fish bones, custard and bits of stale bread fell all over him.

Suddenly there was a gun in his hand. I let the bin go and he staggered about the alley with it down to his waist. The gun was pointing at the ground.

'Wa-hah!' he wailed.

The gun went off and a bullet cracked off the pavement, up against the wall and back again. It only just missed me. I hit the bin with the lid and took to my heels.

After I reported to Sergeant Hammer I dropped the case. As far as I know Stookie never told anyone about what happened. He would be too embarrassed. Apart from telling Hammer I had said nothing either. Stookie would be keen enough to do me harm as it was.

* * *

I walked through to the China Room at other side of the Museum. This was where I had agreed to meet Lindi Lomax. It was filled with glass cases that were lit up inside. Some of them were like wardrobes with

Chinese dresses inside, or suits of strange looking armour. Other display cases were more like desks and they had coins and jewellery laid out inside.

There were only a few others present. An old couple were bent over a case of Chinese dolls. A young man carried a clipboard and leaflets. Over in the corner, standing beside a glass cabinet with shelves, was a woman in her mid-twenties wearing a dark blue trouser suit, looking down at some small statue I couldn't see. She might have been a lawyer or a doctor or someone who worked for the Museum. I stood behind her.

'Ms Lomax?' I asked.

She turned and looked me up and down with a sad, serious expression on her face.

'Mr Hegarty? You're not as tall as I expected.'

'My feet reach the ground and my head never quite scrapes the ceiling. I'm just the right height.'

'We can talk over a cup of coffee,' she said. 'But first, I'd like you to look at this.'

It was a small statue of Buddha carved out of jade, exactly like the one in my desk drawer. Its label said it was 14th century and priceless. It had been brought to this country by a millionaire collector in the late 19th century as one of a pair. The other had disappeared shortly after.

We sat in a corner of the Museum's downstairs café. I bought her a cappuccino and ordered my usual espresso. She still had not smiled. In fact, the muscles of her face hardly moved. She kept that sad, serious expression at all times. I wondered why.

'I have a job for you, Mr Hegarty. I would like you to find the companion to the little Buddha I just showed you.'

'That's a tall order. It's been missing for a hundred years.'

'It was owned by Precious

Emanuel for as long as I was in his home. I know this because I was owned by him too.'

'No one owns anyone else, Ms Lomax.'

'Well, it felt that way. Let me tell you about myself, Mr Hegarty. I come from a well-to-do family but we had a disagreement. I don't want to talk about that. Two years ago Precious Emanuel saw me dancing at the Aurora Club. We went out together a few times. He's a lot older than me, but we fell in love.

'It seemed very natural to move into his flat, provided I could keep working. He agreed but soon decided he wanted me to stop dancing. I felt I needed my own income or I would be nothing more than—I'm looking for the word—a slave.'

'That's a word,' I said. I didn't offer any other words. 'You have a lot to look sad about.'

'Don't read too much into my face,

Mr Hegarty. I wear this expression as a sort of protection. I don't want the men in the audience to get ideas. Also, it dulls the feelings, Mr Hegarty. I think of it as my chloroform.'

'Were you happy with Precious?'

'At first, but feelings between us soon changed. He wouldn't let me go out, far less dance. A few weeks ago he took away my key.'

'You became part of his collection, Ms Lomax?'

'You could say that. When the opportunity to escape came, I took it. I had already packed my bag and hidden it close to the door. When Precious was asleep I slipped out and away. I guessed he would come after me.'

'Even Precious would draw the line at kidnapping. Just the same, he is an unforgiving man. I don't think you've heard the last of him. Where are you staying now?'

'I've moved in with another

dancer. She works as Moondance Eclipse.'

'Do you mind if I ask you something, Ms Lomax? What does this have to do with the jade Buddha we've just been looking at, or its companion?'

'The jade Buddha disappeared from Precious's flat the same night I did. Naturally, he suspects it has something to do with me. I know he is having me followed.'

'Did you steal it?'

'No. It was first stolen a long time ago, but I don't know anything about that. I know it was bought by a gangster called Meyer Lansky in the twenties. Since then it's been handed down. Most recently it was owned by a Chicago gang boss called Tony Tonelli. Precious imports illegal drugs from him. When he learned about the Buddha he asked if it could be included in a deal.'

'If the FBI learn about this it will tie Precious and the Mafia together.

If one falls, both might. So, what do you want me to do?'

'I want you to find the Buddha, Mr Hegarty. I have to get it back to Precious before he does something terrible.'

We left by the front of the building and I waved down a taxi for her.

* * *

My sad-faced client had more to worry about than she realised. Precious would not want word to get round that he had been robbed.

He had to appear untouchable. Otherwise all kinds of small rebellions might happen and they might add up to a fall.

He lived for his collection. For him the statue would have a special value. It would feel as if it was part of him. If the police got to it first he could be charged with dealing in stolen property. Then a lot more charges might follow.

If the Mafia found out it had been stolen from Precious, and it could be evidence against them, they would take a very dim view. The best he could hope for was that they would stop dealing with him. It could be much worse.

I walked alone under the tall buildings that lined the roads back to my office. In my desk upstairs was the very object that was at the heart of all this. I had no idea why it had been sent to me or by whom. What to do? I could play for time and then present it to Lindi Lomax, or to Precious Emanuel. Then again I could turn it in to Sergeant Hammer.

The street was empty as I turned the last corner, or so I thought. As I passed a shop a pair of powerful arms reached around me and a cloth was pressed over my nose and mouth. It was soaked in chloroform. My head spun. I tried to struggle but my legs wobbled beneath me. When I looked down I saw a commando

21

knife tattooed on one of the arms. The words around it said, 'Stookie loves Posh'.

A black curtain came down and I knew no more.

CHAPTER THREE

PRECIOUS EMANUEL

If you have wakened on as many floors as I have you'll know how carpet tastes. Even the best of them is full of dust and grime. Precious Emanuel's carpet was of the highest quality. It didn't taste any better but its thick pile cushioned the blow when Stookie threw me on the floor.

I felt sick when I came round. I was lying on my ear looking across the carpet at a pair of black slip-on shoes with gold buckles. Above them were the trousers of a dark grey, pin-stripe suit. The trouser legs crossed over each other as their owner leaned back in his chair.

'You'd better not throw up,' said a voice from behind me.

'Leave him alone, Stookie.' The second voice sounded from

somewhere above the trousers. It had a foreign accent. 'Can you stand on your own, Daniel? No? Stookie, help Mr Hegarty to his feet.'

Stookie grabbed me under the arms and pulled me up. The man in the seat was Precious Emanuel. He had big, plump hands and a double chin. His long, grey hair was brushed straight back from his forehead without a parting. The suit had a waistcoat with a gold chain across the belly.

'Is it all right to call you Daniel?' he asked.

I nodded.

'Of course, I'm going to have to insist you call me Mr Emanuel. Stookie can just be Stookie.'

We were in a big room, lined with glass cases like the Museum. The cases were filled with small statues, gold coins and jewellery. There were paintings on the wall I thought I recognised—Picasso—Rembrandt—Turner—and at least one modern

24

painter, Peter Howson.

All of them had been stolen. I looked at the Picasso.

'Recognise it?' Precious asked. 'The Nazis stole it during the War. It took me years to locate but it was worth the effort, and the money.'

Evening light was streaming through the window behind Precious's head so it looked as if he had a halo. It also made the silver and ivory in his display cases glow.

'I see you are admiring my collection, Daniel. You have good taste.'

'I've never seen anything like it outside of a museum. You stole it all?'

'Watch your tongue, Hegarty,' Stookie said.

'I prefer the word "acquired",' said Precious. 'I wonder if you really understand what it is to possess such beauty, such value.'

'It has no value,' I said, 'except to whoever sees it. That is to say it acquires more value as more people see it. But you keep it to yourself.'

'Ho ho!' he laughed. 'Well done, Mr Hegarty. You're a clever man. But do you really think every eye is the same?' He rose to his feet. 'Come over here,' he said, turning to the window.

I stood beside him and looked out, and down. We were on the top floor of one of the highest buildings in the city. Skyscraper apartments were all around us, but none was as high as this. On three sides we looked across the city roofscape to distant hills. In the sky were vapour trails from planes.

Looking down we could see the roofs of the city's old buildings. Once upon a time they had been the highest buildings here. In the street far below were people who looked as small as ants.

'Look how tiny the little people are, Daniel. How intent they are on their worthless little lives. Do you really believe they are my equals?'

He didn't wait for an answer. Turning away from the window he pointed at a drinks cabinet in the corner.

'Stookie,' he said. 'Pour me a cognac. Daniel will take a glass of vodka. Won't you, Daniel? Oh, we know all about your little weakness. How long has it been since you took a drink, Daniel?'

'Four years,' I told him. 'I won't take one.'

'Oh come, Daniel. You must be cured by now. One drink won't do you any harm. Will it, Stookie?'

'No, Mr Emanuel.'

'Pour Daniel a glass of the Estonian vodka. It's better than the Russian.'

Stookie poured me a big tumbler of vodka and pushed me into the seat opposite Precious. I put the glass to my mouth and felt the sting. I could taste the vodka, but did not swallow until I licked my lips. Then I wanted more.

'I think Stookie will have to hold your nose for you, Daniel. No, Stookie! Not yet.'

'Why have you brought me here?'

'I'll come to that. Meantime, let's just talk. It's not often I meet with an intelligent listener like you, Daniel.'

'So talk,' I said. 'I'm listening.' At the same time I was looking at the jewelled rings on his fingers, and his diamond cuff links.

'This country has been good to me,' he said. 'A young man can do well if he works hard. I climbed over the Berlin Wall in 1980 and smuggled myself across the Channel. I went to work in a grocery store. Someone came to collect protection money from my employer. Daniel, I wouldn't stand for it! He had been good to me. The fact is they picked on the wrong man. I sent them packing, but not before seeing what a good idea they had. I decided to go into their line of business and soon they were working for me.'

'And you kept on acquiring. I guess it became a habit, Precious.'

'Just so, Daniel, and I made a distance between me and the little people.' He nodded in the direction of the window. 'And so we are here.'

'And at some point you fell in with Big McBride.'

'I'm afraid Big broke the law, Daniel. He's in prison now.'

'I heard you put him there, but that's your worry.'

'You think I worry about Big? Ho! He's one of them, you know; the little people outside the window. He has a brain but no intelligence. He sees no further than the end of his nose. That's why he's in prison.'

'Drink your Estonian vodka, Hegarty,' Stookie said. 'It's good for you.'

'Not yet, Stookie,' said Precious. 'There's plenty of time for that. So Daniel, every so often, from out of the masses, someone special arises.

I'm one. Perhaps you could be too, if it wasn't for your little habit.'

'I don't think so.'

'Oh, don't argue! I know these things. Ms Lindi Lomax is also such a person. I would visit the Aurora Club and watch her while she danced. Why did you meet with her today, Daniel? Does she feel she needs you to protect her from me? I do hope not. I wouldn't hurt her for the world. Well, perhaps for the world. Did she mention a small idol? Something has gone missing from this apartment. Have you been keeping it for her? That's what I suspect, Daniel.'

My blood froze. If Precious sent Stookie to my office and he found the Buddha he would kill both Lindi Lomax and me.

'And where would you keep such a thing, Daniel?'

'I don't know what you're talking about.'

'Stookie followed you into the

Museum. When he saw you speaking with Ms Lomax you were in the China Room looking at a jade Buddha. It used to have a partner over there.' He pointed to an empty shelf in one of his display cabinets. 'When Stookie saw you together he called me. Now, what do you have to tell me?'

'Nothing.'

'Do you know what I really want, Daniel?'

I looked at my feet and said nothing.

'No answer? Well, what I really want is to have both the jade Buddha and Ms Lomax back.'

He leaned forward in his chair, put his glass to his nose and inhaled.

'Mm,' he said. 'Perfect. Like her. Did she tell you how she danced among my art for me? No? Oh Daniel, the way she moved across that very carpet! Her skin was as smooth and perfect as the surface of that little idol. Yes Daniel, I want them both back, but most of all the jade Buddha. Where is it?'

'I don't know what you're talking about.'

'Stookie?'

Stookie pushed me back into the seat and grabbed me by the nose. With the other hand he forced the glass of vodka into my mouth. At first I had no choice but to swallow. After that I took it because I wanted to. I took it because I am an alcoholic and had been four years without a drink. I finished the bottle because I wanted to. I guzzled it down.

They kept questioning me but I didn't tell them anything. Eventually Precious crouched beside me.

'I want the Buddha brought to me,' he whispered. 'If I have to find it for myself I will personally kill whoever has it. Remember that, Daniel.'

The last thing I heard was the two of them laughing as I passed out.

Then I felt myself hoisted over Stookie's shoulder and carried downstairs. He drove me back to my office and left me. It was after midnight. I sat on the stairs and sang myself to sleep with an old Rod Stewart number.

CHAPTER FOUR

AN OFF DAY

I woke sitting on the pavement with my back to the wall. It was 4:00am and cold. I was still drunk. When I looked down I saw a small pool of vomit. Some of it was on my jacket. I had guilt feelings at being drunk again. It was time to go home to bed.

I didn't have far to go but it took me a long time to get there. Inside the flat I hung my jacket behind the door and staggered past the bathroom to my single room. In one corner was my single bed. In another was the cooker. I had lived here for three years. The flat I rented before had been larger, but this was cheaper.

How had I come to this? Once I had a marriage and a family. Now I scraped a living from minding other people's business.

Dermot had to get through university somehow. He worked in a bar at nights, but it wasn't enough. When I paid Marie what she was due this was all I could afford. Now it all seemed pointless. If I could have taken another drink I would have done so right then.

I boiled the kettle and made a cup of tea but left it to cool on the sink. Somehow I got out of my clothes and crawled under the duvet. I put my mobile phone on the table by the bed and tried to sleep. I dreamt of Stookie Frampton with the bin over his head, and Precious Emanuel whispering in my ear.

'If I have to find it for myself . . .'

*   *   *

Traffic noise started again about 6:00am. I decided then that I would give Precious his idol and get off the case. Why should I care about his criminal affairs or his collection? Come to that, why should I care about Lindi Lomax? Drinking again was a much more attractive prospect.

I felt terrible, but experience told me I would recover. Mind made up, I fell asleep again. The phone woke me about mid-day.

'Daniel, are you all right?' It was Sugar. 'Where are you anyway? Someone is here to see you.'

'I'm at home. I won't be in today. Do I have an appointment I've forgotten?'

'I'd say this one just dropped in on spec.'

'No more appointments, Sugar. No more cases. I'm quitting the business.'

'If you say so, but . . .'

I hung up.

I could not get back to sleep. My head was still going round and I felt as if I might be sick again. A few minutes later I went for a pee, then I had to sit down. I was sitting on the

WC in my underpants with my head over the sink when the front door pushed open and Dermot came in.

'Dad?'

'Don't look,' I said.

It was too late. He was at the bathroom door.

'Okay Dad, it's like that, is it? I'll go through and wait for you. If you want a shower let me know. I'll stand by so you don't fall.'

I showered without help and asked Dermot to pass through a clean shirt and jeans. There was no point dressing for work. Dermot made tea and I managed to drink some. We sat in opposite chairs by the gas fire.

'That was me Sugar called about. I wasn't going to make an appointment with my own father so I walked round here. I'm sorry you're drinking again, Dad.'

How do you tell your son you were kidnapped by the most dangerous thug in the city, threatened by the most powerful gangster, and finally had a bottle of Estonian vodka poured down your throat?

'Don't ask what happened. You won't believe it.'

He's not quite as tall as I am, but Dermot is broader in the shoulder. He takes after his mother. This is good. It means he is better looking and may have missed the alcohol dependency gene.

'I looked in the fridge,' he said. 'I could scramble some eggs for us— put them on toast.'

'I'd like that.'

Dermot made the eggs and we ate by the fire. The boy could cook. I wished he had learned it from me. Over coffee I asked why he had come round.

'I sent you a note that I'd left home. You and Mum don't speak to each other so I wanted you to know I haven't fallen out with her. It's just I wanted to be a bit more free. The flat I share is closer to the university, but it's also closer to here. Mum said

I shouldn't look you up. If you weren't drinking now, you soon would be.'

'And this is how you find me.'

'Dad, can I help?'

'No. It's up to me.'

'My flat's just on the other side of the park. If it helps we could see each other more often.'

'You're a good boy,' I said.

'If you ever need to—you know—talk through anything, I'll be there.'

'You're a fine young man.'

'DON'T speak that way!' He was angry with me. There were tears in his eyes. 'I'm trying to get through to you. Oh, this is pointless.'

'No,' I said. 'No, it's not. It's a good thing you've done. Coming here, I mean.'

I looked around for something to give him. There was nothing. There was only Dermot and me, a pot of tea and no place to hide. He had seen the worst of me but he hadn't either run away or come out punching. I loved him with all my heart but couldn't find the words to say it.

'We can meet more often,' I said. 'I'd like that. Your mother won't be keen though.'

He looked at me oddly. 'You could be wrong in that. She says she remembers you as a good man.'

'Who is this Karen you're sharing with? I bet Marie doesn't like her.'

'They've never met. Karen's just a friend. We're doing the same course. Her parents own the flat and my rent helps pay the bills. She's okay.'

Later we walked through the park together. I left him at the bridge the Gordon Water flows under. We stopped and looked for a while. The river flowed as it always had. So, I thought, father and son—someone to live for.

'Dad,' he said. 'I know you're living in that squalid hole so I can get an education.'

'Your mother works. She pays too.'

'But you pay most. And you have so little. I want you to know I appreciate it. I'm working to do well. I'm going to make my life a success.'

We hugged by the park gates and both of us spoke at once. People looked but we didn't care.

'Be strong,' we said at the same time.

I took the rest of the day off. Deep down, I wanted a drink. This was what Precious and Stookie had done to me. They had broken my will not to drink. That one bottle of Estonian vodka was enough to cancel four years on the wagon. Other things had happened though. It was the thought of Dermot that stopped me. He had made me stronger than any of them.

I would go back to work.

*   *   *

Sugar was at her desk when I got in to the office next morning. She was

41

playing some game on the internet. The time she wastes really annoys me.

'Shouldn't you be filing or something?' I asked.

'My nails?' she replied.

At my desk I turned on my computer and deleted an extra day's spam. Dermot's letter still lay on my desk. There was another envelope lying beside it.

'Any messages from yesterday?' I called through to Sugar. 'Anyone drop by?'

'Snitch left that letter on your desk.'

I opened Snitch's letter. It said, 'Just to let you know that Big McBride will be out in six weeks.'

There would be war between Big and Precious. That was for sure.

'Anything else?'

'Your new client, Ms Lomax, called. She wanted to know if you were getting anywhere.'

I thought about my overnight

decision to present Lindi Lomax with the jade Buddha. Yes, I thought, she would be safer if it went back to Precious Emanuel. After that, she could refuse his advances. I didn't think he would be desperate enough to kidnap her and keep her against her will.

On the other hand, we could turn it in to the police. There might be a reward. Of course, Precious might come after us. He would not want to lose face in the underworld. His friends in America would be looking on. They would not like to see the Buddha's history being investigated any more than Precious would.

It was a problem.

I got up and closed the door so Sugar wouldn't see. Back at my desk I opened the drawer and took out the little box. It was heavy in the hand. I opened it and took out a glass paperweight. Inside was a house with a reindeer beside it and a sleigh. I turned it over and a storm of snow swept around the scene. The jade Buddha was gone.

CHAPTER FIVE

THE AURORA CLUB

Since no one had been in my office but Dermot and Snitch the thief must be one of them. I did not believe it could be Dermot, so it must have been Snitch.

Sugar told me he had been on his own when he delivered the letter. He was carrying a brown bag. It looked like it had something heavy in it.

He must have brought the Christmas paperweight with him. The jade Buddha would have taken its place in the bag when he left. He must have replaced the idol with the paperweight in the hope that I would not open the box. When I felt the weight I would think the little idol was still in there.

Only the original thief could have known I had it. That meant Snitch was the original thief, or it was someone he was in cahoots with.

So, why had it been sent to me in the first place and who by?

The obvious answer was to get it safely out of the way for a few days. When the thief felt it was safe he would pick it up again. Who stole the jade Buddha was still a mystery but Snitch Mitchell was in it up to his long nose.

I speed dialled 'Simon Martin' but it rang out. Snitch wasn't answering.

I decided I would tell Lindi Lomax what had happened. Perhaps by putting our heads together we could come up with something. I called her and we agreed to meet at her place of work that night.

*   *   *

The Aurora Club was only two streets away from the Museum. It was 10:00pm when I arrived. The Club's name was lit up in neon and

46

so were the names of the two artistes who were appearing that night: Moondance Eclipse and Dolores. Dolores was the stage name of Lindi Lomax. She had told me to look out for it. Moondance was the friend she was staying with.

I paid my way in and hung up my coat.

The Club was part casino, part bar and part strip joint. It was smaller than it looked from the outside. When I entered I saw the clientele were almost all men. Some of them had girlfriends or wives with them and everyone was pressed very close together.

The first part you came to was the casino. There were tables for blackjack and dice, and a roulette wheel. The roulette wheel was the busiest. You had to pass the gambling area to get in or out. This meant you went past it twice and were more likely to spend money there. It was gambling that made the

Club's profit.

A sign said that all mobile phones should be turned off. I did so and pushed my way to the roulette table. From here I could see across the room.

In the middle was the stage area. It was raised and brightly lit where the rest of the place was dark. The stage was square with a pole reaching up to the ceiling. Obviously this was where Dolores and Moondance Eclipse would perform. There were chairs all around it but at this time both stage and chairs were empty. The girls were to come on at 11:00pm.

On the far side of the room was the bar. The drinks in the Aurora Club were very expensive. It was not the sort of place a serious drinker would choose. The clients had to have plenty of money and most dedicated boozers are very poor, as I am. It was busy though. The first person I saw was Stookie Frampton.

He must have felt my eyes on him, because he turned and looked at me. Then he gave a mocking little laugh and turned to lean on the bar.

I saw something else that was of interest. Another man was watching Stookie, someone who looked just as tough as he was. I have followed enough people to recognise when someone else is doing it. This man was looking at Stookie but didn't want to be seen doing it. His drink looked as if it was not alcoholic, and he hardly touched it. He had not noticed me, but I would stay clear of him.

Lindi Lomax had told me not to go into her dressing room before the first show—afterwards would do—so I waited by the roulette table. Since it had the biggest crowd I would not be noticed.

At 11:00pm a man wearing a dinner suit appeared on stage and announced that the dancers were coming on. They would perform for an hour and be on again at 1:00am.

Lots of men and a few women sat down to watch. I sat at the back of the audience and waited until Moondance Eclipse arrived. She entered from a door beside the bar. That must be the dressing room, I guessed. The audience roared so loud I was almost frightened by them.

Moondance wore a spangled dressing gown that she dropped at the side of the stage. After that she was wearing almost nothing: a thong, a tiny brassiere and high, spiky heels. When the music began she smiled and raised both hands in the air.

The music was just a recording; there were no musicians. The man in the dinner suit turned the base line right up.

THUMP! THUMP!

Moondance stepped confidently across to the pole and grabbed it. She leaned back so far her hair swept the stage. When she lifted one leg in the air and straightened it the crowd roared again. All the men leaned forward in their seats. I couldn't take my eyes off her. It was not so much that she was sexy, although she was. It was the way she took over the whole room. She turned and leaned against the pole with her arms around her and wiggled down until she almost reached the floor, then she rose again, slowly.

I looked across the stage and saw Stookie in the front row on the far side. He was drinking in Moondance's performance, loving it. Towards the end she took off her brassiere, held it over her head and stood smiling at her audience for just a moment. Then she picked up her dressing gown and ran from the stage.

The man in the dinner suit came back. It was time for Dolores to appear. There was an even bigger roar of approval. Obviously she was a great favourite and had her regular fans.

Like Moondance she dropped her gown on the stage and strode to the pole. Once again the music started.

THUMP! THUMP!

Lindi Lomax had a slimmer figure than Moondance. She was also a better dancer. When she ran her hands down her sides and leaned forward I had to look away. I knew her. This made her different.

Unlike Moondance, she wore her sad, serious expression throughout her act. I knew she used it to keep her distance from the audience, but it didn't work for me. It didn't work because I had spoken to her, I knew her. It didn't matter that she was almost naked.

She wore her face like a mask. Anyone looking at her face would think she was broken hearted. I glanced around. Probably I was the only one there who had even noticed her face.

Now I saw her expression in a

different way. In the Museum she had called it her chloroform. Now I could see what she meant. She used it to protect herself on stage, but it stayed with her all the time. In a way what she did was heroic, but she paid a price. I wondered what price Moondance Eclipse paid. Beneath her smile she might be sad too, or hurt, or disappointed, or angry.

Because I could not look at Lindi Lomax, or Dolores, while she danced, I looked across the stage at the crowd. Stookie was in the front row. He seemed to be laughing quietly at her—she must have seen him. Standing further back was the man I saw earlier. Like me he wasn't watching the dancer. He had his eyes on Stookie.

Then I saw something else. Stookie was not looking at Lindi any more. I followed his gaze as he rose to his feet. He had been following her to see what, or who, might turn up. Last time it was me. This time it was a man who was taking a blue handkerchief from his coat pocket. He blew his nose and wiped it three or four times to bring it to a shine. He was wearing his raincoat and baseball cap and must have been the worst dressed man in the place.

He also had a brown bag that he clutched to his breast.

I shouted, 'Snitch, watch out!'

Snitch stood up as Stookie climbed across the seats towards him, pushing people aside. Men started shouting. Some of them tried to leave in a hurry. When Stookie reached into his jacket and produced a gun Lindi put her hands to her mouth and screamed.

I jumped onto the stage and dragged her towards the dressing room. She lifted her dressing gown from the floor as we passed.

'Snitch!' shouted Stookie. 'Don't move or I'll shoot. I want to see what's in that bag.'

Snitch wasn't wasting any time. He

pushed his way to the front door as we made for the dressing room. As he shouldered his way past I could see there was something green in it. Of course it was the Buddha. He made it to the door just as I pushed Lindi into the dressing room. I stopped for a moment and looked round.

Stookie was standing on a seat while all around him people were throwing themselves to the ground. He pointed his gun at Snitch's disappearing back. Suddenly the chair toppled underneath him and he fell back. The gun went off and the bullet embedded itself in the ceiling straight above him. A piece of plaster came loose and fell on his head. The last I saw of him his two big feet were resting on the back of the chair while he lay moaning on the ground.

I closed the dressing room door behind me. Moondance Eclipse was already dressed. She gathered Lindi's clothes and pushed them into a bag. 'Come on,' she said. 'It's time to leave.'

Another door opened onto the street. Moondance unlocked it and we rushed through. She had a car waiting outside. It was a small hatchback with only two doors. 'Get in,' she said to Lindi. 'You too, Mister.'

I opened the passenger door and pulled the seat forward. Then I pushed Lindi inside just as Moondance started the engine. She drove off as I pulled it shut behind me.

From somewhere along the main road we heard the sound of a police siren.

CHAPTER SIX

THE RETURN OF THE JADE BUDDHA

Moondance took us to her flat on the edge of town. It was a lot bigger than mine though not as big as the home I had shared with Marie. Lindi Lomax was still in costume but she went into her bedroom to change. She said she was more embarrassed now than with the whole audience watching.

When she came back she was in jeans and tee shirt. She looked good, and her expression was less serious for once. It was as if a load had been taken from her shoulders.

'I've seen some fights in bars,' said Moondance, 'but that was the scariest! Did you see the guy with the gun? Let the police sort it out. If they want us the management can tell them where we live.'

Suddenly we were laughing and very jolly. I suppose it was the release of tension. Moondance had a drinks cabinet in the corner. She opened it and took out a bottle of malt whisky. 'It's all I drink,' she said. 'Want some, Mr . . . ?'

'Hegarty. Call me Dan.'

I was so relaxed I almost forgot I don't drink. Moondance poured whiskies for the two of them and I had a cup of tea. We settled down by the fire.

'What a great showbiz name,' I said. 'Moondance Eclipse, did you invent it yourself?'

'In a way,' Moondance said. 'It came after someone said my bottom is too big and it sort of stuck.'

'It was a jealous rival,' Lindi said. 'Actually, it was me before we got to be friends.'

'Your bottom looks okay to me,' I said. I felt myself blush. 'I mean— not that I was looking.'

'Why not?' Moondance asked. 'I'm

an exotic dancer. You're supposed to look. Anyway, she said it was big enough to blot out the sun.'

'Now I'm embarrassed,' Lindi said.

I decided to change the subject.

'I wanted to tell you. Someone sent the jade Buddha to me. I don't know who.' I didn't say it had arrived before I met her in the Museum. 'Later, Snitch stole it again when I was out of the office. I'm pretty sure of that. The question is: what was he doing in the Aurora Club with it?'

'Why not call him and ask?' Moondance said.

'He's not answering his phone. My only guess is that he was trying to get it to you, Lindi. Stookie was following you in the hope that something would turn up and lead him to the idol. When he saw Snitch with the bag he put two and two together.'

'Why would Snitch give it to *me*?' Lindi asked.

I did not say what I really thought;

that they were in it together. I suspected that Lindi Lomax had taken the idol with her when she escaped from Precious Emanuel. She probably thought he owed it to her after all she had given him.

She couldn't keep it so she got Snitch to post it to me. When she felt the time was right she sent him to get it back. That was why Snitch was in the Aurora Club with the jade Buddha in a brown paper bag. He was going to give it back to her and, eventually, take his share of the spoils.

Secretly I liked this. I thought she was clever and brave. Perhaps Precious Emanuel did owe her something. I looked out of the window at the city. Snitch and the jade Buddha were out there somewhere. 'Let's just hope he stays clear of Stookie Frampton,' I said.

By now it was almost 2:00am. Moondance let me sleep in the lounge. In the morning she gave me a lift back to my flat and left me there.

*   *   *

I climbed the stairs with the strange feeling that something was wrong. I was right. My front door was hanging off. Suddenly my heart was in my mouth. What if they were still inside waiting?

As I passed the bathroom I saw the cistern lid had been taken off. In my room all the clothes had been stripped from the bed. The fridge door was open. So were the doors under the sink. My wardrobe and chest of drawers were all open and the contents thrown about. No one was there. They had done their work and left. Whoever they were they were looking for something small enough to fit in the cistern, or a drawer. It was the jade Buddha, obviously.

I looked at my watch. It was

11:00am. I pushed my clothes roughly back in their drawers, fixed the bed and replaced the cistern lid. Then I returned to my office.

Sugar looked up from her desk as I entered. This time she really was filing her nails.

'At least you're doing something useful,' I said. 'You won't catch them on the keyboard when you're playing patience.'

I sat at my desk and looked at the Christmas paperweight. How ridiculous it seemed. Suddenly I remembered I had not turned my mobile phone back on since I entered the Aurora Club. It turned out I had missed two calls. The first was from Dermot. The second was from 'Simon Martin'. Snitch had tried to get through. I was about to call Dermot when Snitch called again.

'Dan, I'm outside your office. Let me come up, please. I'm hurt.'

'Let you? There is no one I want

to see more right now.'

In a minute Sugar opened the door and Snitch limped in. He was in a terrible state. His shirt was torn open. His coat was filthy and covered with footprints and he had lost his baseball cap. For some reason I had not noticed before that his hair was grey. Worst was his face. The right side was bruised and swollen and the eye was closed. The damage looked fresh. His skin was so pale I guessed he was in shock.

'Sugar,' I called through. 'Bring a cup of hot tea for Mr Mitchell. Put in plenty of sugar.'

I waited until he had the cup in his hands before asking what happened after he ran from the Aurora Club.

'I just kept going. I couldn't let them get the idol.'

'So you did have the jade Buddha in that bag. You stole it from this drawer, didn't you Snitch?'

He nodded.

'Where is it now?'

He answered through swollen lips.

'I couldn't let them find me with it. I posted it to someone. Then I hid for the night. I didn't go home in case they were waiting. This morning I went round to your flat to see if you were there. I met Stookie coming out. He hit me on the head and bundled me in his car, but first he kicked me about. Then he took me to Precious and between them they did this.' He pointed at his face.

'Did you tell them who you'd posted it to?'

'No, but they found the recorded delivery in my pocket. When they let me go I tried to call you. You shouldn't turn your phone off for so long, Dan.'

'What are we going to do with you, Snitch,' I said. 'You're your own worst enemy. You should have given them the thing and saved yourself the pain.'

'It's priceless.'

I almost said, 'So are you, Snitch'.

But only Sergeant Hammer and I had any real use for him. Not many would think he was priceless. He took out his handkerchief again and blew his nose painfully. Gobbets of blood came away. When he tried to polish his nose it was just too tender.

'Who did you send it to, Snitch? We'd better warn them.'

'The only address I could think of was the one on your desk.' He pointed at Dermot's letter that said he had left home. I read it when you were out. I thought it would be safe with your son. Between us we could work something out later.'

'You sent the jade Buddha to Dermot?' Goose bumps of fear rose on my skin.

Sugar appeared at the door. 'Is everything all right?' she asked.

'No it's not!' I shouted. 'Snitch, if anything happens to him . . .'

Now I guessed why Dermot had called. I called him back.

'Hi, Dad,' he said. 'You'll not guess

what I've got here.'

'Yes I will. Where are you?'

'I'm on my way to the Museum. Someone sent me a funny little idol. It's like a little green Buddha. I'm going to see if it means anything to them. It might be valuable.'

'I'll say it's valuable. Where are you?'

'I've just crossed the bridge in the park.'

'Not far from the Museum then,' I said. 'Look around you Dermot. Is anyone following?'

'It's pretty crowded, Dad. I don't think so.'

'Did you call the Museum first? Is someone waiting for you?'

'Yes, the China curator.'

'Just keep going. I'll meet you there. Whatever you do, don't turn back.'

'Dad . . .'

'Just keep going. If you see anyone suspicious don't stop to pass the time of day. I'll get there as quick as I can.'

'Sugar, call Sergeant Hammer!' I opened my drawer. 'Tell him I'll meet him with Precious Emanuel's jade Buddha at the Museum just as soon as he can get there.'

'Anything else?'

'That should bring him at the run. And running, Snitch, will be the quickest way of getting there. Are you fit for it?'

'I can hardly walk.'

'Well, we'll walk as quickly as you can manage. But it might feel like a run. Just one more thing before we go.'

From the drawer I took my Colt Police Special and its box of bullets. I loaded five of the revolving chambers and left the other empty for safety's sake.

CHAPTER SEVEN

IN THE CHINA ROOM

I ran all the way while Snitch lagged behind. All I could think of was Dermot with Stookie Frampton knocking lumps out of him.

As I approached the Museum I saw Precious Emanuel climbing the stairs. Dermot would be inside by now. I could call him again but I was breathless and it would take up time.

I pushed through the swing doors and made for the China Room. When I entered, Precious was facing Dermot and another man. This must have been the curator. Dermot held the jade Buddha in both hands in front of him. I dodged behind a stone column and listened.

Precious took a gun from his pocket and pointed it at Dermot.

'Just step forward and put it on

68

this display case,' he said. 'Put it down carefully. That's it. Now, step back and join your new friend. Both of you put your hands up.'

Precious looked down at the idol and his eyes widened with greed.

'Mine again,' he said. He ran his hand across it, speaking to it almost as if it was a child. 'The little people don't deserve you.'

'Now Mr Dermot Hegarty,' he said. 'If there was only one of you I could take the jade Buddha and simply walk away. But you've brought a witness, so I can't do that . . .'

The curator swallowed deeply.

'I wonder how tomorrow's headlines will read?' said Precious. '"Meddling student found dead in Museum"?'

I already had my gun in my hand. I stepped out from behind the column. I was side on to Precious so he would have to turn to get a shot off at me. I would be too quick for him.

69

'Think again, Precious,' I said. 'Now, drop your gun on the floor.' He hesitated. 'DROP IT!'

Precious Emanuel's gun clattered on the marble floor.

'Now kick it away.'

The gun slid across the floor between us. He turned and looked at me.

'So,' he said. 'The little people are ganging up on me. Do you seriously think you can get the better of Precious Emanuel?'

'When the police look into that hoard in your flat they are going to make a lot of connections,' I said. 'My guess is you'll go to prison for a very long time.'

My heart almost stopped when I felt the barrel of another gun against my neck. Too late, I realised Precious had been distracting me. Stookie had crept up behind.

'Your turn, Dan,' he said. My gun clattered at my feet. 'Now kick it into the middle.'

I kicked it and it slid across the marble floor to rest beside Precious's gun.

'Now go and stand beside the others with your hands up.'

I stepped across to stand beside Dermot and the curator. The curator was trembling with fear. No one could blame him, but Dermot was calm. His eyes ranged from side to side and I could see he was wondering what he might do. I was proud of him.

'Play for time,' I whispered. 'Don't give them an excuse.'

'Three of them,' said Precious. 'That's a lot to kill at once. Let's get them closer to the back door where we can make a cleaner getaway.'

Precious picked up the jade Buddha and tucked it inside his jacket. Although it made a bulge no witness would be able to identify it in future.

'You heard the man,' Stookie said to us. 'Bunch together and ...'

'That's enough,' said a gruff voice. This voice had an American accent and came from somewhere behind Stookie. Its owner had stepped into the China Room from the Japan Room next door. I recognised the man who had been following Stookie in the Aurora Club. He was carrying a machine pistol that could take us all out in a single burst. Stookie looked as if he was going to turn quickly and take a chance.

'I wouldn't do that, Stookie,' I said.

'The man's right,' said the stranger. 'This weapon cuts people in half. Drop the gun.'

Stookie's gun clattered on the marble floor.

'Now kick it into the middle of the room.'

Stookie's gun slid across the floor to rest beside the other two.

'Now Precious, put the jade Buddha back on the display cabinet and go stand beside the others.'

Precious took the idol carefully

from inside his jacket and put it down. Now there were five of us standing together with our hands up.

'How are you these days, Precious?' said the stranger.

'A bit fretful over the Buddha, Tony,' said Precious. 'But business is good and I have few rivals, so I am otherwise well.'

'Really? You haven't been worried about what your ex-girlfriend might have to say to the police? I think you should have been, Precious. My friends in Chicago have been talking about it. We feel our whole British operation is threatened by her and Meyer Lansky's little hand-me-down.'

'There's nothing to worry about, Tony,' said Precious. 'I have it all under control.'

'Tony?' I asked. 'Antony Tonelli?'

'I've been following Stookie for the past week,' he said. 'It was never difficult. I watched him watching you and the stripper. After the Aurora

Club I watched him put the boot into your talkative friend. I could have taken him out at any time but I had to get the idol back. There is a lot to be lost if the police use it to link us up. The American operation would have been threatened too.'

He put his hand on the jade Buddha.

'You can't be too careful about little things,' he said. 'I'll be on my private plane in an hour. Destination: Florence. From there I'll be flying to Afghanistan to negotiate over a poppy field. Now, boys, it's all over. Say goodbye to your bodies.'

He slipped the safety catch on his pistol to 'off' and pointed it at us.

'Think again, Mr Tonelli,' said a female voice.

I looked over my shoulder. A woman's arm had appeared from around the column beside us. It was dressed in a blue pin-stripe sleeve and the hand was holding a small pistol. It couldn't do half the damage that Tony Tonelli's machine pistol could, but one bullet would be enough and it was aimed at his head.

'Drop the gun!'

Tony Tonelli's gun clattered on the marble floor.

'Now kick it away.'

The machine pistol slid across the floor to rest beside the other guns.

Lindi Lomax and Snitch stepped out from behind the column.

'Hello, Dan,' said Snitch. 'I called her to say what was happening.'

'All of you,' said Lindi. 'Stand beside the display cabinet.'

We all shuffled across to join Tony.

'Stand on the side away from the Buddha. That's it. Keep your hands up. Now, Precious and Stookie, step away from the others.'

Precious and Stookie looked at each other. They were frightened.

'STEP ACROSS!'

'Don't shoot, Ms Lomax,' Stookie begged. 'Please.'

'We're going to have a floor show,' said Lindi Lomax. 'Precious, this is for all the times you humiliated me in your flat. It's for calling me "Dolores" in private and making me dance to Stookie's old Spice Girls' albums. Take your clothes off!'

'You came willingly, Dolores.'

'I didn't stay willingly. And don't "Dolores" me. Now STRIP! No one else move.'

Precious and Stookie took their clothes off down to their underpants and socks.

'That's enough,' she said. 'Precious, you're even fatter than I remember. And Stookie, you have too many tattoos. Now Precious, this isn't just for me, it's for all the little people you think are beneath you. Mr Tonelli, do you know "The Stripper"? I mean the tune.'

' "The Stripper"?'

'Yes, it goes like this—Dada dad aa-ah! Dada dad aa-ah!'

'I guess so.'

'Well sing it—all of you. Sing it!'

One by one we started up and soon we were all singing together. 'Dada dad aa-ah!!!'

'LOUDER!'

We sang at the tops of our voices. 'DADA DAD AA-AH!'

'Now Precious, you can dance to my tune. You can too, Stookie.'

They started by hopping up and down on the spot.

'Jump higher,' she said. 'Swing those bottoms! C'mon, let's see you grind.'

'Aw, Dolores,' Stookie moaned.

When she fired a shot close to their feet they jumped out of their skins. They kicked their legs in the air and turned round to twirl their bottoms at us. Precious put his back against the display cabinets and wiggled down into a squat the way Moondance had against her pole.

The curator was first to giggle. Then Dermot started to laugh out loud. Soon we were all laughing our heads off. People who heard came through from the other rooms. Soon we were part of a big crowd. All of them were laughing at the two ridiculous gangsters. The little people were all laughing. Perhaps Precious didn't think other people were so little any more.

'Now stop,' said Lindi. 'The fun is over. You know how it feels.'

Precious looked at her with hatred. 'Okay Dolores,' he said. 'Are you going to use that thing?'

'The gun?' she asked. 'You know Precious, I think I will.' She pointed it at him and took aim.

'Put that gun down,' said a voice. It was Sergeant Hammer. Sugar's call must have got through. Suddenly the room was filled with policemen.

'Don't shoot, Ms Lomax,' he said. 'There is no need. Drop the gun and kick it into the middle of the floor.' Hammer looked down there for the first time. 'That's quite an arsenal,' he said.

'No need?' said Lindi. 'I don't think Mr Emanuel has suffered enough. Not yet. Brace yourself, Precious.'

'No!' Precious dropped to his knees and begged. 'Please don't kill me.'

'Funny how often it goes like this,' said Tony Tonelli. 'When it comes to the end they all beg. I guess we are all little people.'

'I've always loved you, Dolores,' said Precious.

'Love? Me?'

Lindi Lomax pulled the trigger.

'No!' Precious cried, and fainted as the Buddha exploded beside his head.

It broke into four large pieces and a thousand tiny white fragments. It was only green on the outside. Inside it was white because it was made of plaster of Paris. It was not jade after all. It was a fake.

CHAPTER EIGHT

ENDINGS AND BEGINNINGS

About two months later I stood looking out of my office window. It was mid-afternoon and men were going in and out of the Grove Bar. Some of them came out quite drunk. Once I would have been one of them. I might be again.

I returned to my desk and the newspaper. The front page was all about Precious Emanuel and the jade Buddha. It was a big joke that his empire was coming apart over a piece of plaster. Sergeant Hammer was getting a lot of credit.

When he entered Precious's flat he found millions of pounds worth of stolen art. After that he gained entry to all kinds of records and was soon able to prove that Precious was involved in drugs, protection and many other crimes. The connection to Antony Tonelli's Mafia family was also established. The FBI became interested and soon it seemed as if half the criminals in Britain and America were being put away.

No one knew what had happened to the real jade Buddha but most thought Meyer Lansky had made the switch in 1932 to prevent the American tax agency getting their hands on it. No one knew where it was now.

At that moment the phone rang. Business calls all came through on Sugar's extension. When my phone rang first it meant it was a personal call.

'Hi Dan.'

It was Moondance. After Lindi moved into her own flat I called her and we went out a few times. She liked going to the movies or for a pizza. She said, 'With my job I see enough of clubs and drinking. Really what I want is to stay in and be homely.'

I thought I'd like to try that. I bought a bottle of wine for her and some expensive, tasty coffee for me. She hadn't been in when I called so I left a message on her voice mail. 'Let's have that night in tonight?' I had suggested.

'Get my message?' I asked.

'That's why I'm calling. Dan, I'm not available tonight or tomorrow night.'

'That's too bad. We can always do it next week.'

'What I'm trying to say is—you're a lovely man. I've enjoyed our time together. I like you and I'll always respect you, but I know you want to settle again and I'm not ready.'

'Settling is the last thing on my mind.' Too late, I realised I was putting up an argument.

'A pole dancer isn't good enough for you, Dan. This is the sex trade I work in.'

'That doesn't make you a . . . Ah,

forget it.' Of course she was making an excuse. It wasn't about her job or me being an alcoholic. We just didn't quite fit together and pretending otherwise wouldn't change it. Deep inside, I was still married to Marie.

'I understand,' I said. 'But listen, we're still friends. Okay?'

'Always.' She hung up.

Sugar looked in. 'Your appointment has arrived. Are you all right? You look a bit shaken.'

'Appointment? I'd forgotten. Who is it?'

'He says he's an old friend. And Ms Lomax is with him.'

'In that case I'm available.'

'Hello, Daniel,' a voice boomed from behind Sugar. It was Big McBride. Lindi Lomax came in behind him carrying a large shopping bag.

When Big sat down his chair looked as if it had been built for a doll's house. 'Long time no see,' he said.

'You know each other?' I asked.

'Laura is my niece,' Big said. 'She spent a lot of time visiting me in prison while I was thinking what to do about Precious Emanuel.'

I looked across the desk at her. 'Big is the family you broke off from?'

'That's right,' she said.

As usual her expression was sad and thoughtful. 'After my parents died Uncle Big brought me up. When I went through my teenage rebellion I decided I would do the last thing he wanted me to do.'

'Become a pole dancer.'

'Hur hur,' Big laughed, shaking his head. 'My little Laura—a pole dancer.'

'About the time Precious started showing an interest Uncle Big made contact again.'

'I was in prison,' Big said. 'In there you get to thinking about things. Regrets, Dan, you know?'

I looked at Laura, or Lindi, or

Dolores, or whatever she was called. 'Does this mean you had it all planned from long ago?' I asked.

'When I went to live in Precious's flat I had a purpose. The whole idea was to take something that he would hate to lose. Your guess was right, Dan. I stole the jade Buddha.'

'Except it was a plaster Buddha,' I said, but she let that pass.

'I gave it to Snitch and he sent it to you.'

'All this was planned by me,' Big said. He sounded very pleased with himself.

'Then he made sure you knew about the Buddha, even though it had already arrived in the post.'

'Let me get this right,' I said. 'Big encouraged you to join the Precious Emanuel establishment even though he knew what would happen there?'

'I can take care of myself,' she said.

'I know that. Did you get Snitch to steal it back as well?'

'That's right,' said Big.

An ugly thought was forming in my head. 'He wasn't supposed to get caught, was he? That was an accident. But the ticket that showed the Buddha had been sent to Dermot . . .'

'We'd have made sure they knew about that somehow,' said Big.

'And told me?'

'You wear your heart on your sleeve, Dan. You would have gone to protect your boy with that pea-shooter of yours.'

Big had wanted me to shoot Precious, either to protect Dermot or in revenge for his killing. In prison he would have the best possible alibi. My stomach turned at the way he had used his niece but a second thought told me she had been as tough as he was. I didn't know her after all.

'You're looking at me a certain way,' she said. 'Like most men you're afraid of strong women. Learn to live with it, Dan. I've rejoined the family business and things won't be the same again.'

'Laura takes after me,' said Big. 'But listen, the reason we tell you all this is because we want you to join us. Not outright, of course. We just want you to stay close to your friend Sergeant Hammer. He has a future and maybe we can use him again.'

'Did Snitch know about this all the time?' I asked.

'Don't be too hard on him,' said Big. 'He never really understood what it was all about. All he wanted was to save Laura from Precious and Stookie. Hur. Hur!'

'What's so funny?' I asked.

'Laura told me about Precious and Stookie dancing. I'd rather they were dead but—humiliated and in prison will do.'

'You should leave now,' I said. 'I might be a low down drunk but I'd never put someone I love in danger. You'd have seen Dermot killed and not blinked. At least you didn't get the idol.'

'Show him, Laura.'

She reached into her bag and lifted out the jade Buddha.

'Just to let you see it this once, Dan,' she said. She placed it on my desk so the chubby little green man and I could look into each other's faces.

'No one but the three of us even knows it really exists,' she said, smiling.

'For the first time since I've known you,' I said, 'you've smiled. I think I prefer you without it. You just look hard.'

They left with the Buddha and from my window I watched them drive away. The future wasn't hard to read. Big McBride was back in charge but his successor was already in place and Lindi Lomax—I'll use her real name now, Laura McBride—was even colder and harder than he was. Somehow I could live in the same town as Big, or Precious and Stookie, but thinking of Laura made my blood run cold.

Looking into the street I saw a familiar figure enter the Grove Bar. There was no mistaking the old coat and baseball cap.

'You can stop work for the night, Sugar,' I called to her. 'Work— remember that? It's what you did before you came here.'

'That was called marriage,' she replied. 'See you in the morning.'

I waited until she was gone before locking up and walking across the street. Walk? I almost ran. I could get as drunk as I liked. There was no Moondance to look forward to, no one to go home to and no future. Why not get smashed?

There was no point in being angry with the likes of Snitch either. 'What will you have?' I asked.

'I . . . uh . . . I . . . uh . . . a pint!'

'Me too,' I said. 'Barman, let's have two pints of beer for my friend and me, and I'll have a vodka for mine to chase down. After waiting so long on the shelf it might need the exercise.'

'You don't need this,' said Snitch.

'Don't go telling me what I need. For a start I need friends who are on my side. That's not you and it's not sad-faced Lindi-Dolores-Laura or whatever her name is. Sadly, it isn't Moondance Eclipse either. I have only one friend I can truly rely on and our bartender is pouring him as we speak.'

'Vodka isn't your friend, Dan.'

'Blah blah,' I said as my mobile phone rang. It was Dermot.

'Dad, it's like this. I told Mum how you saved my life. She asked me to call. She wants to have a cup of coffee with you in the Museum café—she says you can show her where you held a gun on Stookie Frampton. Say "yes", Dad.'

I turned off the phone with plenty to think about.